Couch Detective

Book 2

James Glass

Copyright James Glass 2020

© 2020 by James Glass
All rights reserved. No part of this book may be reproduced, stored in a retrieval system, or transmitted in any form or by any means without the prior written permission of the publishers, except by a reviewer who may quote brief passages in a review to be printed in a newspaper, magazine, or journal.

James Glass

The final approval for this literary material is granted by the author.

Couch Detective

First digital version

All characters appearing in this work are fictitious. Any resemblance to real persons, living or dead, is purely coincidental.

Print edition produced in the United States of America

Checkout my other Books
Fiction

Mark Wheeler Crime Thrillers

Things Left Behind

Whisper Creek

Rebecca Watson Crime Thrillers

Stone Cold

Minutes to Midnight

Kestrel Hitman Series

The Kestrel

You Solve It Chapter Books

Couch Detective Book 1

Couch Detective Book 2

Non-fiction

The Ultimate Chief Petty Officer Guidebook

Author's Note

As you read each of the stories in Couch Detective, it's this author's recommendation that the reader doesn't read more into the story than what is written. If you do, then you might find yourself following clues that may or may not be there.

But if the case leaves you clueless, don't worry. I've added a hint at the end of each story. If the hint doesn't help you solve the case, don't worry. The answers are provided at the end of each chapter.

Read the story, gather the clues, and solve the case. And have some fun while you're at it.

This book is dedicated to all the true couch detectives out there. You know who you are.

Chapters

1. The Interrogation
2. Clue
3. Deadly Campers
4. There's a Dead Man in my Soup
5. Dead Body
6. Believe it or Not!
7. Hunting Accident?
8. The Meeting
9. The Stolen Baseball Cards
10. Death at a Funeral
11. Case of the Stolen Headdress
12. Suicide or Homicide?
13. The Story
14. Running Man
15. Death of a Salesman

16. The Phone Call

17. The Hitchhiker

18. Brothers

19. The Juror

20. The Case of Mistaken Identity

21. Death of Betty Jo Davis

22. The Case of the Stinky Shoes

Chapter 1

The Interrogation

Homicide Detective Donald Hunt sat across the table from newly widowed Kelly Cochran. Her husband, Johnny, had been gunned down by an unknown assailant less than four hours before.

Hunt was known for his ability to see through the lies people told every day. After thousands of interviews and interrogations he'd become a human lie detector. And he was fairly certain Mrs. Cochran was lying through her teeth. Well, if she had any to lie through.

He decided to go over the interrogation a second time. Maybe he'd missed something.

"Where were you and your husband going to at nine o'clock at night?"

"To the store to buy some smokes."

"Smokes for who?"

She sighed. "I told you this already. For me."

"And why did your husband tag along?"

"Johnny doesn't like me walking by myself after dark." She smiled, revealing a toothless grin. "Thinks I'll get raped or something."

He winced from the visual. The unpleasantry of seeing her naked might drive him to drink a few beers tonight.

Stay focused and find the lie. It's in her statement somewhere.

"So, it was you who decided to get cigarettes?"

"For the umpteenth time, yes."

He needed to drag this out if possible and see if he could get her to slip up. "Just bear with me a little longer. What was the name of the convenience store?"

"Majik Market."

"Did you notice anything out of the ordinary?"

"Like what?"

"Perhaps a possible suspect or witness?"

She waved a hand. "Nah. Nothing like that. But I remember the moon was really bright tonight."

"How so?" He wondered why she waited until now to bring this up. Maybe this line of questioning would lead somewhere.

"I don't know. It reminded me of that song Amoré. You know. About how big it is like a pizza pie or something like that. I'm horrible at remembering limericks."

"I think you mean lyrics."

She rolled her eyes. "Whatever. Anyway, I remember walking toward the moon and being hypnotized by the wondrous glow. I must have really been in a trance, because out of nowhere this shadow formed from behind me and swallowed me up. The shadow seemed to stretch on forever. Like a spider with these long tentacles."

"You mean long legs?"

She laughed. "Can you imagine spiders with tentacles?"

Hunt shrugged. Then he gestured for her to continue.

"We turned back and saw this guy wearing a black mask. He aimed the gun at Johnny and demanded money.

"Johnny tried to reason with the guy but got a bullet between the eyes instead. Poor Johnny. He deserved better."

Hunt looked at her. The woman liked to talk. Mostly gibberish but he knew the truth lay inside the blurry lines she called a statement.

"You got a smoke?" Mrs. Cochran asked. "I could really use one. Especially, after everything I've been through."

This woman was stone cold.

"I don't smoke. And even if I did, there's no smoking inside the building."

She sighed. "Can you at least tell me when I'll get the life insurance? Johnny was the breadwinner."

"You'll have to contact the insurance agency. I'm sure you'll need to file a claim."

"Can I go home now?"

Hunt stood. "Give me a few more minutes."

She crossed her arms. "Fine. But can you get me a soda?"

"Sure."

Hunt walked back to the video room and decided to watch the interrogation he just recorded. Thirty minutes later he found the clue he was looking for. He hadn't missed it during the first interrogation because she hadn't mentioned it until the second go around.

Did you find the lie?

Hint: The shadow.

Kelly Cochran stated she was walking toward the brightly lit moon. If this were the case, her shadow and her assailants shadow would have cast behind her. Not in front like she stated.

Chapter 2

Clue

Detective Rebecca Watson entered the lobby of the hotel. A tall, thin woman stood next to her partner, Tony Francisco. The woman wore a sport coat several sizes too large. Her long, tanned legs attracted the attention of several men standing idly by. Water dripped from her hair.

"What do we have?" Watson asked.

"Appears to be a murder-suicide."

The woman sobbed. "It's horrible. So horrible."

Rebecca nodded at Tony who returned the gesture. He'd remain here and finish the questioning while she checked out the scene.

***

The room was a sea of activity as Crime Scene Investigators canvassed the area for evidence. The drapes were drawn over the window. Fluorescent lighting from a lamp next to the king size bed supplied a pseudo-dawn atmosphere.

Ray Soriano, the medical examiner stood near the body in the bed.

Rebecca approached him. "Is that the husband?"

Ray scratched his balding head. "Good morning, Detective. I see you're lovely as ever."

Rebecca flashed a smile as she moved toward the body.

Ray pointed with an index finger. "Meet Mr. Plum. He was killed by Miss Scarlett with a revolver in the bedroom." He let out a boisterous laugh. "Get it, the game Clue."

Rebecca rolled her eyes. "Why do I even bother to ask?"

He chuckled again then continued, "Gary Plum here was shot five times in the chest with a .38, courtesy of Mrs. Plum."

Rebecca looked down at the body. Gary Plum, a white male looked to be in his mid-thirties lying on his back, eyes at half-mast.

His lips were pulled back from clenched teeth, almost in a sneer. There was blood on his cheek, nose, and chin, most likely coughed up as he died.

The front of his white robe, now saturated in blood, fanned out from his body. Because of this, Rebecca could see the bullet entry points into the man's chest.

Ray tapped her gently on the shoulder. "The wife's in the bathroom, a single shot to the head." His voice softened. "Tragic."

Rebecca glanced in the direction of the bathroom then turned her focus back to the body on the bed. "Tragic, indeed."

She thanked Ray and headed to the bathroom. When she entered, Mrs. Georgia Plum was on the white tile floor. The tiny woman lay in a pool of blood, her long brown hair matted. The .38 revolver was next to her left hand. She wondered if the wife found her husband here in bed with Bambi downstairs and in a fit of rage, Georgia shot him before killing herself. It certainly looked plausible.

"What's the consensus?" she heard her partner ask from the

doorway.

She turned her head and looked up at Francisco. "Appears to be a murder-suicide. Did you perform a GSR test on Little Miss Sunshine downstairs?"

Tony smiled. "Getting a bit jealous, are we?"

Rebecca ignored the statement.

"Yes, came up negative."

Rebecca turned her focus back to the corpse. "Bring me up to speed on her statement."

Tony took out a small notepad and flipped through a few pages. "Sally Sutton is Mr. Plum's secretary at his business. He owns Plum Construction. Apparently, he and Sally started having an affair six months ago. The wife had no clue, even when he worked late nights and an occasional weekend."

He flipped another page. "Mrs. Plum spent most of her time at church gatherings and volunteer work for various charities. Sally said, Gary was quite the looker and always up for a challenge, both personally and sexually. This weekend marked the married couple's tenth anniversary and he wanted to introduce the two women and have a ménage à trois."

Rebecca simply nodded. She wondered if Gary had any idea his bonehead decision would backfire. She let the thought pass as Tony continued.

"Sally checked into the room next door. Gary texted her on his cell saying he and Georgia were going to the pool for a swim. While they were out, she would gain access through the door that connected the two rooms. His instructions were for her to lie in bed with nothing on. When they came back from the pool, he would lead his wife to the bathroom where they would take a quick shower together and then enter the room. He knew Georgia would be surprised but said he could get her to agree with the threesome. Appears things didn't go as planned."

"No shit."

Tony grinned. "When he tried to explain his fantasy to Georgia, she became so infuriated with the notion she ran into the bathroom and locked the door. Several minutes later, she came back out holding a gun in her right hand. After a brief argument, she shot Mr. Plum repeatedly. Then she pointed the gun at Sally and pulled the trigger, but it was empty. That's when Sally rushed out of the room still naked and ran downstairs to the lobby. She approached the front desk and told them to call nine-one-one. Afterwards the clerk gave her a sports coat to wear from lost and found."

"I guarantee she'll think twice before sleeping with another married man."

Tony agreed.

Rebecca turned to walk away when she realized this wasn't a murder-suicide. Sally Parker was a cold-blooded killer. And she almost got away with the perfect crime.

How did Rebecca solve the case?

In Sally's statement, she said Mrs. Plum had come out of the bathroom holding the pistol in her right hand. Yet, the .38 was located next to the dead woman's left hand.

When Rebecca arrived at the hotel, she noticed Sally's hair was dripping wet. She'd stated she ran out of the room after Mrs. Plum tried to shoot her, but the gun was empty. If she'd done so, how could her hair be wet, unless she'd taken a shower, which would have also washed away the gunshot residue.

The final clue is when Sally stated Mrs. Plum tried to shoot her, but the gun was empty. The .38 revolver holds six rounds, not five.

Chapter 3

Deadly Campers

Officer Timothy Simmons arrived at the Blackwater campgrounds ten minutes after noon. He'd been dispatched to investigate the death of a camper.

Sunshine warmed his cheeks as he exited the vehicle. The temperature hovered a few degrees above seventy.

Two RVs were parked along the campground. The closest one faced east, the other north. Empty beer cans littered an area where a campfire had been burning. Smoke wafted from the ashes.

The door of the nearest RV swung open, and two men appeared stepped onto the landing, one after the other. Both men staggered down the steps.

One of the men stood over six feet, with mangy hair. The second was short and plump. Both appeared to be in their early forties. And they reeked of alcohol.

"Glad you're here, Sheriff," Mangy said. "Some guy got mauled by a bear."

Simmons was certain this hadn't been relayed in the nine-one-one call. Otherwise, the game warden would've been dispatched. He thought about calling this in but decided it could wait until he determined if what Mangy said was true. After all, there was no telling what the man saw in his drunken stupor.

All three walked along a dirt trail. Simmons noticed the sandy path was covered with a variety of shoe and boot prints. He didn't see any animal tracks. When he turned back, the two men were struggling to keep up.

The three men continued down the path for about another hundred yards before coming to a bicycle lying on the ground.

Next to the bike lay a man with half his head missing. By all appearances he'd died from buckshot and not at the hands of a bear.

"Do either of you know this man?" Simmons asked.

"No," Stocky said. "He arrived late last night. This morning he hopped on his bike and sped away. Several minutes later, I, um, uh, heard him scream. When I ran to see what happened, he was dead."

Simmons nodded, but the man's story didn't sound altogether true.

"Did either of you see the bear?" Simmons asked.

Mangy kicked at the sand with his boot. "No but we heard the damn thing. Scariest noise in my life." He raised his right hand as if taking an oath. "If I'm lying, I'm dying."

"That's true," Stocky agreed. "If Gary hadn't decided to ride his bike this morning, he'd still be alive."

"Yeah," Mangy said. "Poor bastard never had a chance."

Simmons stared at the body of the deceased. This was no bear mauling. Even he knew this. But without any incriminating evidence to substantiate these two knuckleheads were involved, he couldn't arrest them.

He'd turned back to call in the crime scene unit when he realized the men made two mistakes.

Did you find them?

Hint: Look at the dirt trail again.

The two men stated they didn't know the deceased. But Stocky slipped up and called him Gary. How could he know the man's name? The bicycle was their second mistake. There were no tire tracks in the sand indicating a bike was ridden along the path.

Chapter 4

There's a Dead Man in my Soup

Detective Sarah Pratt parked the unmarked cruiser in the long, spacious driveway to the massive Tolliver mansion. She'd arrived thirty-three minutes after the 9-1-1 call came in.

Pratt approached the portico and knocked on the large oak door. Insects buzzed around the overhead light.

The door swung open and a buxom blonde wearing a black tube dress and sporting four-inch heels stared down at her.

Pratt showed her shield.

The woman flinched, but quickly regained her composure. "Why are you here? My husband had a heart attack. No one murdered him."

Interesting choice of words.

"I've been called because someone has died. It's standard operational procedure for a detective to determine if a crime has been committed."

Pratt wasn't telling the entire truth. Normally the medical examiner would decide based on their findings. But her boss had sent her to investigate, and that's what she intended to do.

Blondie waved a hand in the air. "That's fine. I don't have anything to hide."

"Can you show me where the deceased is, Mrs. ...?"

"Tammy Tolliver."

They walked down a long hallway to the kitchen. Then they veered to the first room on the right. At the head of the dining room table was a man slumped, his face buried in a bowl of what appeared to be split-pea soup. Next to the bowl was a glass of water.

A tea kettle whistled on the stovetop.

"I'll get that," Mrs. Tolliver said and walked away. A moment later she reappeared with a cup of tea. Steam wafted in the air.

"Can you tell me what happened?"

"My husband died."

Pratt despised this woman, who'd been confrontational ever since arriving on scene. But being a bitch wasn't a crime.

"What I meant to say is were you present when your husband died?"

"Yes."

"And?" Pratt prompted, but this woman wasn't offering any information.

The woman gave a reluctant sigh. "We were sitting down having dinner. Danny didn't won't the chicken cordon blue, so he made himself some soup."

"Did he get up or do anything else before he died?"

Tammy tapped the side of her teacup with a polished, red nail. "Yes. He wanted a cup of tea, so he went to the kitchen and started the kettle."

"Okay. What happened next?"

"He returned to the table and began eating his nasty, split-pea soup. Why anyone likes that disgusting-looking liquid is beyond me."

"Then what?"

"He simply fell into his soup. A bit ironic if you think about it."

Pratt didn't find death funny at all but decided to ask anyway. "How so?"

She snickered. "Waiter. There's a dead body in my soup."

This woman had a weird sense of humor, but without any evidence, Pratt couldn't arrest her for murder. And that's if one had even taken place.

Then she realized the woman had lied. She didn't know if Tammy Tolliver killed her husband, but it would require further investigation.

What lie did Tally Tolliver tell?

Hint: Tea

Tammy Tolliver stated her husband got up to make tea. But the kettle whistled after Detective Sarah Pratt arrived.

Pratt arrived thirty-three minutes after the 9-1-1 call. A kettle takes anywhere from five to fifteen minutes to whistle which can only mean Tammy is the one who started the kettle.

Chapter 5

Dead Body

Detective Charley Pearson parked behind the ambulance at the curb outside of Hoagies Heroes. The sandwich shop was a local favorite. Now he wondered if a dead body inside the establishment would be bad for business. Then again, the town gossip might boost sales. He'd seen it before. Not that it mattered to him. Pearson wouldn't be eating here anytime soon. If ever.

The front door had been propped open, but a city police officer was standing inside the entryway, a clipboard in hand. The deputy jotted Pearson's name and badge number before letting him pass.

Two tables still had food and beverages, which had been

abandoned by their customers.

A dead body lay slumped across the seat of the booth. John Doe had eaten half of his sandwich and most of the chips on his plate before getting the call from the Grim Reaper.

Pearson used an app on his cell to take the man's fingerprints. With any luck John Doe was in the system. Several minutes later, the results came back to the man's identity. Bobby Jones, aka the Ghost, had been a hitman for the mob. Now someone had whacked him. Or so it appeared.

Pearson stared at the glass of water on the table. Condensation ran down the sides, which looked out of place. Not the condensation, but the fact this man had a glass, instead of a paper cup. He wondered if the man received special perks for being someone of stature, although he wasn't sure. He didn't believe it to be a wise decision for the Ghost to announce himself. Especially in a public establishment.

Pearson continued to search for clues as to who the killer might be. The problem is he didn't see any outwardly signs of the man's demise. No bullet holes, strangulation, or stab wounds. Nothing to indicate murder. Poison appeared to be the only logical choice. And that's if this is how the man died.

One thing did appear odd. If the Ghost ate so much food, why would the glass still be full? They didn't have a wait staff here to refill drinks. And why the glass cup?

There were still too many questions and not enough answers. But this was the way investigations worked. First was the pursuit of countless dead ends. Next you add the colossal chunks of wasted time and energy. Then throw in the many obstacles along the way. You mix it altogether and the truth is in there somewhere.

But Pearson feared his case, like the body of the Ghost had gone cold before he even got started. Someone wanted this man dead, but who?

The glass appeared to be the single thing out of place, therefore the only clue to work with.

Pearson kneeled and moved toward the man's lips. He took in the faint scent of bitter almonds. He stood and waved a crime scene tech over named Valerie Swanson.

"Can you test to see if the victim was poisoned with cyanide?"

"Sure can," Swanson said. "It'll take a moment to get set up."

The tech removed a small, black device about the size and shape of a printer cartridge from her crime scene kit.

Then Swanson pricked the Ghosts finger, like a diabetic would do to measure blood sugar, and placed the sample into the cartridge device.

Pearson walked into the kitchen to kill time as he waited on the results. Maybe he'd get lucky and stumble on another clue. Before he reached the door, Swanson announced, "Positive for cyanide."

"Great. Now all I need is a suspect."

Swanson smiled. "Sorry. Can't help you there."

He nodded and walked to the officer standing at the front door.

"Did you get the names of the customers and employees when you arrived on scene?"

He pointed to another officer standing outside. "Johnson has them over there."

"Thank you."

Pearson approached Johnson. "Can you give me a quick rundown of the players here?"

"Sure. There were five customers when your John Doe collapsed. A husband-and-wife dining at a booth and three sailors at another table."

"How many employees?"

"One. Apparently the other called out sick tonight."

Pearson figured he was grasping at straws, but one of them might be his killer.

He approached the husband and wife. "What can you tell me about the deceased?"

"Not much," the wife said. "We'd just sat down to eat when the man collapsed. One of the three men sitting at a table near us rushed over to check for a pulse. When he didn't find one, he got the attention of the guy working behind the counter to call nine-one-one."

He asked the couple several more questions which didn't reveal anything to solve the case.

Next, he decided to talk to the employee.

"What can you tell me about the deceased?"

"Patrick comes in about once a month."

"His name is Patrick?" Pearson figured the man used an alias since he wouldn't want his real identity known.

"Yes. Or at least that's what he told me. Why? Is that not his real name?"

"Just trying to get an identity. We had him listed as a John Doe for the moment. Did he ever give a last name?"

"Not that I ever recall. He never really talked too much. Mostly kept to himself."

"Does he use the same booth every time?"

"Yes. The Ghost isn't too keen on sharing."

"And did he always get a glass instead of a paper cup?"

"That's Patrick for you. Only the best for that guy. We may not be a ritzy restaurant, but we do what we can when we can."

"Did you notice anything out of the ordinary tonight?"

"Other than Patrick dying, no."

"Thank you."

"Hope I've been helpful."

Pearson thanked him again and made his way to the three sailors.

"Did any of you notice someone sitting with the deceased?"

One of them said, "Only the dude making sandwiches."

"Did he stay long?"

A second guy said, "They chatted for a bit, until the man and woman came in. He got up and went behind the counter to get their orders."

"Do you guys come here often?" Pearson asked.

The third guy said, "At least three times a week."

"Have you ever seen the deceased here before?"

All three shook their heads.

Pearson didn't know what else to say. The investigation was running cold. He was about to leave when he thought of something. "Did you see the employee bring anything out to the deceased?"

They seemed to think about the question. Two eventually shook their heads. The third said, "Yeah. He brought the man a fresh glass of water."

One of the others snapped his fingers. "That's right. I only remember because when he left to meet the two customers, he grabbed the man's empty glass from the table."

Pearson thanked them. He figured the empty glass might

contain the cyanide. Or at least that was his theory. But theories weren't evidence. As he made his way toward the kitchen, he realized the employee unwittingly identified himself as the killer.

Did you uncover the clue?

The employee may have known Bobby Jones as Patrick, but he slipped up when he referred to him as the Ghost.

The only way the employee could have known Jones was the Ghost is if he knew who the man's real identity.

Chapter 6

Believe it or Not!

Mike Collins sat at his desk reviewing his notes. The private investigator had been hired by an insurance company to investigate a potential fraudulent claim.

The plaintiff, Mrs. Peabody, claimed she'd wrecked a rental vehicle due to the car having faulty brakes which caused her severe whiplash. She was suing for pain and suffering.

The insurance company had the car checked out by three different automotive shops. Two didn't find anything faulty, but the third reported the brake fluid reservoir was low and might have contributed to the accident.

Collins sipped the last of the coffee and contemplated getting another cup. The caffeine barely kept his eyes open as it was, but he needed to keep going. Being a private investigator didn't pay well. At least not for him anyway.

He stood and stretched his six-foot frame. Collins yawned as he scanned the tiny office cluttered with files. Too bad he couldn't afford a secretary.

There was a knock at the door.

"Mr. Collins. Are you in?" a female voice asked.

The hour wasn't late, but he hadn't expected anyone. Then again, it could be a potential client.

When he opened the door, a beautiful young woman in a yellow sundress and matching sandals stood in the hallway. The neck brace she wore was a bit of a distraction until he caught sight of her blue eyes.

"My name is Crystal Peabody. And I'd like to hire you."

The insurance firm had never sent a picture of Mrs. Peabody, so he'd assumed she'd be old and wrinkly. He glanced away, trying not to ogle.

"Sorry. I can't. Would be a conflict of interest."

"Can I at least tell you my side of the story?"

He turned to her. "I've been briefed already."

She gave a warm smile. "What if we drive to the scene. There's no harm in that is there?"

He wondered what her angle was. There had to be one for her to come see him. The only thing which made any sense was she needed him to be on her side.

Then again, it didn't take a private investigator to figure that one out.

He was about to decline the offer when he realized she might provide some evidence that could sway his decision. At this point in his investigation, he couldn't prove who was right or wrong.

He nodded. "I can't see the harm."

"Thank you. We'll take my car if you don't mind."

"Sure."

Several minutes later, he was sitting shotgun in a Mercedes Benz. He'd never ridden in a high-end vehicle.

Her GPS came on and told her to take the first right.

"You don't know where we're going?" Collins asked.

"No. The night of the accident I was going to a new restaurant in a part of town I've never been."

They drove for thirty minutes talking about a variety of topics. He learned she was recently divorced. The husband left her for his personal secretary. He also learned she'd been lonely and depressed since the divorce. She was planning on meeting someone at the restaurant the night of the accident.

"I don't recognize this route," she said slowing down.

"You've only driven this way once. Plus, the GPS might be taking us on a different route."

"You're probably right."

"Did you and your ex have kids?"

She shook her head. "No. I'm thankful for that at least." She paused. "You ever been married, Mr. Collins?"

"Divorced twice."

"Children?"

"Nope."

"Guess we're both destined to live alone."

They approached a hill. Before they reached the top, Mrs.

Peabody swerved to the shoulder and as they descended the hill, avoided a pothole.

They continued another five minutes until they reached a fork in the road. She slowed and pulled onto the grass.

"This is where the accident occurred. My GPS was giving me a fit with redirecting. So, I decided to stop until the problem resolved itself. But when I pressed the brakes, the car never slowed."

She began to sob.

Collins felt bad for her and really wanted to be on her side. He ran the events from earlier as he tried to reconstruct the scene.

That's when he realized Mrs. Peabody made two mistakes tonight. Both proved she lied.

What are the two mistakes Mrs. Peabody made?

Hint: Take another look at the GPS.

The first mistake is when Mrs. Peabody shook her head. If she suffered from severe whiplash, she wouldn't be able to.

The second mistake is when she stated she didn't recognize the route. If this were true, then how could she know there would be a pothole on the other side of the hill.

Chapter 7

Hunting Accident?

Detective Royce Mosley arrived at Whisper Creek a quarter past three. He parked the sedan behind two pick-up trucks with a variety of hunting stickers on their bumpers and back windows. An SUV was parked ahead of the two trucks.

Instead of getting out right away, he placed his hands against the heater vents a bit longer. This winter season had been brutal. The entire month of January never reached temperatures above zero.

Mosley exited the car and began his trek down a deer trail. The cold stung his lungs with each breath he inhaled. His boots crunched in the snow.

After twenty yards he came to a small clearing. Two men

huddled together. One was about three inches taller than the other, but each of them wore woodland cammies with an orange reflective vest.

Then there was the body lying face up. Crimson sprayed across the snow surrounding the victim. He didn't notice a blood trail, so the man died where he was shot.

Hunting season always produced injuries, but this was the year's first casualty.

Mosley approached the two men. He retrieved a small recorder from his coat pocket to record their statements.

"What are your names?"

The bigger of the two said, "I'm Sam Gates and this is my cousin, Frank Johnson."

"And the victim?"

The cousins looked at each other, then back to Mosley. He thought he recognized fear in their faces. Then again, their reaction may have been from the dead body nearby.

Sam said, "Don't know him."

Mosley thought of checking the decedent's pockets for identification but decided it better to wait for the coroner to arrive first. Until then he'd continue his investigation.

"Can either of you tell me what happened?"

Sam cleared his throat. "We both arrived before sunrise. Wanted to get an early start."

"That's right," Frank said.

"How did you guys arrive?"

Sam stared at him as though he'd asked a stupid question. "We drove our pickups."

Mosley thought about asking about the SUV but decided to wait and see if they brought it up.

"Did either of you see anyone else?"

They shook their heads.

"How did you come upon the deceased?"

Sam sighed. "I think I need a lawyer."

"No, you don't," Frank said. "It was an accident."

"But I shot a man."

"Not on purpose."

Mosley listened as the two continued to argue back and forth. He could've stopped the conversation due to Sam requesting a lawyer, but since he wasn't asking any questions, he didn't see any harm in letting the two squabble.

Sam sighed. "Fine. I'll tell him what happened."

Mosley held up a hand. "So, you don't want a lawyer?" He needed to get this on record. This way what was said before now should be admissible in court.

"No. I don't want a lawyer."

"Okay. What happened?"

"I was in my tree stand over there." Sam pointed to the east and Mosley could see the unobstructed view of the stand which was about twenty feet up the tree.

Sam continued, "The sun had been up for about half an hour or so when I heard a rustling noise coming from where we're standing now. Because there weren't any other hunters in the area, or at least that's what I thought, I shot blindly into the bushes. The man came into view, staggered several yards then collapsed."

"And you don't recognize him?"

"Never seen him before."

Mosley could tell Sam was lying, but he couldn't prove he

shot the man on purpose. After all, they said there wasn't anyone else around, which hadn't been true. Otherwise, his John Doe would still be alive.

"And you're certain there wasn't anyone else around?"

Frank kicked some snow on the ground. "We were the only two out here. There weren't any other hunters or vehicles when we arrived."

Mosley nodded and shut the recorder off. He turned and studied the deer stand. These two knuckleheads were spewing lies, but he needed proof.

Then he studied the body. Both men had lied and now he could prove it.

Did you catch their three lies?

    Hint: Review the vehicles and the tree stand. If this doesn't help, take another look at the body.

When Detective Royce Mosley arrived, he noticed three vehicles. Two pick-ups and an SUV. Since the trucks were parked behind the SUV, they would've known someone was already there.

Sam said he shot the man, blindly. But Mosley had an unobstructed view from the tree stand to the victim. This was murder and not an accidental shooting.

Sam also stated the man staggered, but Mosley knew this was a lie. There wasn't a trail of blood.

Chapter 8

The Meeting

Elizabeth Perkins only had one goal in life—to make partner at a prestigious law firm. After eight years of sixty-plus hour weeks, the blood and sweat finally paid off. She'd been tipped by a source that a meeting had been scheduled at the home office of Sheldon, Patterson, and Levine to announce the new partners.

Perkins pulled her eight-year-old Honda in front of a two-story white stucco building. The car had been a present from her late father after passing the bar exam. Although she could afford something more extravagant, the sentimental value was priceless.

Dark clouds reflected in the ocean blue floor-to-ceiling windows. The marquee read Sheldon, Patterson, & Levine, P.A.

Attorneys at Law.

Perkins walked through a set of double doors that automatically opened. The foyer was a spacious lounge filled with couches, recliners, and cushioned chairs. Several flat-screen televisions played sports and movies at either end of the lobby. The place resembled a resort instead of a law firm.

As she approached the receptionist behind a large oval pine desk, a man in overalls accidentally dropped a metal bucket. White paint spilled onto the dark, marble floor. The man cursed at himself as the puddle continued to spread.

"Ms. Wilkes, will you keep people from stepping in this mess? I'll be right back to clean it up."

"Sure thing, Rodney."

Rodney scurried off.

Perkins approached the counter, avoiding the paint on the floor. She informed the receptionist of her meeting and was told to take the elevator to the second floor, then walk down the corridor to the last door on the right.

Perkins thanked her and left.

The frosted glass door was propped open when she arrived, and several dozen people were already inside the spacious office. Paul Sheldon, the lead partner of the firm sat behind a huge oak desk, his feet propped up on the corner, smoking a cigar. The smell was sweet, which Perkins welcomed. Sheldon nodded at her and she gave a small wave. She was finally going to become a partner. The excitement coursing through her veins was electric.

She started toward him, but he stood and made his way to his personal restroom.

Ted Nash, another partner walked over, and they embraced in a quick hug. The two had been intimate at one time, but now remained friends. He'd also been the one who informed her about the meeting today.

Everyone mingled about the room sipping brandy, wine, or champagne. Some ate hors d'oeuvres from silver platters.

No one seemed to be in a hurry to announce the new partners and Perkins was content. She simply enjoyed the moment thinking life couldn't get any better. Her talents were finally being recognized and her dream would soon become a reality. She wished her father were here to share in her success.

A trim, good-looking man approached. "I'm Hunter Smith."

She introduced herself and the two shook hands. "I'm making partner today," Smith said.

"Me too."

"Cheers," he said. The two clanked glasses. Smith spilled some. "Sorry. I'm a klutz."

"No worries. Could happen to anyone."

"No. Just me. I stepped in some paint in the lobby on my way up. How's that for luck. Good thing I'm an excellent litigator otherwise I'd be screwed."

Perkins didn't know what to say, so she remained quiet.

After an awkward silence Smith excused himself.

Perkins saw that Sheldon had returned. The man leaned against his desk and tapped a gold letter opener against a bottle of what appeared to be brandy. The conversations around the room ceased. He took another toke from his cigar then exhaled a puff of smoke.

"Thank you all for coming to this meeting."

Someone in the crowd said, "We didn't have a choice, Mr. Sheldon."

There were a few chuckles.

"Announcing new partners is one of the best parts of my job. Each of you have achieved remarkable things for us and we're successful because of your talents."

He studied the room. When his eyes fell on Perkins, the electricity flowing through her veins returned. She wanted to scream with joy, but she maintained her composure.

Sheldon took the bottle from his desk and poured a healthy dose into a snifter. "There are six of you in this room, each of you ready to take on the world. But we only have five spots open this year."

Several people gasped. One of them had been Perkins. Surely, she'd be one of the five. She had to be.

"There are a number of ways we can do this. Draw straws. Pick a color. Play rock, paper, scissors."

The last drew some laughs but Perkins didn't find it funny. Nausea began to set in. She wanted to throw up.

"This year will be a bit different. The person who arrived last, will be the one who is kicked off the island."

Everyone stared around the room trying to figure out who'd been the last to arrive. In fact, Perkins wondered if it had been her. She hadn't noticed anyone entering after her, but she hadn't paid any attention.

Sheldon sipped his brandy then stood atop of his desk. "I need the six nominees to step forward."

A moment later, Perkins moved in line with four men and a woman.

Sheldon pointed with his stogy, nestled between his index and middle finger. "Who is the unlucky soul?" He smiled. The man clearly was enjoying this spectacle.

"Elizabeth Perkins, you are the last contestant. Thanks for playing. Better luck next year."

Tears filled her eyes as the crowd laughed. Her dream had become a nightmare. The five others broke away receiving handshakes and pats on the back from everyone in the room.

Ted approached her and the two embraced.

"I'm sorry," he said. "Guess I should have drove you. Then you wouldn't have been last."

She nodded. Then a thought occurred. "I wasn't the last to arrive and I can prove it."

How can Elizabeth Perkins prove she wasn't the last to arrive?

Hint: Paint.

When Elizabeth Perkins arrived at the lobby, the man in the coveralls spilled paint on the floor.

Hunter Smith said he'd stepped in paint in the lobby. If this were true, he arrived after Perkins. But Paul Sheldon wouldn't have noticed Smith's late arrival, because he entered his personal restroom shortly after Perkins walked in.

Chapter 9

The Stolen Baseball Cards

July 10, 2019

Returning from a swim at Stony Creek, nine-year-old Perry Winkle pedaled his bike down Main Street. When he turned onto Stapleton Road, he glanced over his shoulder and saw McKenzie Callahan following him on a bike.

She gestured with her right hand for Perry to stop. So, he pulled onto the grass next to the side of the road.

"What do you need?" Perry asked. He didn't know what the local bully wanted from him. Surely not to hire him for a case. After all, who in Pleasantville would dare commit a crime against McKenzie?

Then he wondered if he did something to make the girl mad. Mad enough to beat him up. Maybe he shouldn't have stopped, but it was too late now. His heart raced as McKenzie got off her bike and walked toward him. "I need to hire you. Someone broke into my clubhouse and stole my baseball collection."

She handed the neighborhood sleuth a card.

Perry looked at it. On the front was a picture of a man in a baseball uniform. The name on the bottom read Johnny Bench. He flipped the card. On the back were statistics. They recorded his batting average, hits, homeruns, on-base percentage, and other stats during his baseball career.

Perry handed it back.

"Who is Johnny Bench?"

McKenzie gasped. "You don't know who—" and stopped mid-sentence. She shook her head. "And you call yourself a detective. Johnny Bench only happens to be the greatest catcher of all time."

Perry nodded as if he understood, but really didn't. He never watched baseball. Sometimes he watched football on Sundays with his dad, but that was the extent of his knowledge of sports.

McKenzie reached into her pocket and pulled out a wallet. She took out two dollars and handed it to Perry. "I'm hiring you. So, when do we start?"

"I need to go home and change clothes. I also need to get some things. This type of operation calls for a little spadework."

McKenzie shrugged. "I have no idea what that means."

"It means we need to do some digging around."

"You mean like with a shovel? My dad won't like that. He has a perfectly manicured lawn and would get mad if we start digging holes in the backyard."

"No. It's a metaphor. We need to find a connection between the baseball cards and why someone would want to steal them from you."

"I don't know what metaphor means, but as long as we don't ruin the grass, I guess it's okay."

Just then, it started to rain. It was an afternoon shower, which came like clockwork on most days. It started around 2:00 p. m. and lasted about ten minutes.

Perry got on his bike. He wiped the wetness from his forehead with his palm. "I will meet you at your house."

Twenty minutes later, Perry knocked on the front door of 129 Melancholy Lane. He was holding a black canvass bag which contained his notebook, magnifying glass, flashlight, and the rest of his detective kit. The door opened and McKenzie appeared.

She gestured Perry inside. They walked down a long hallway. The hardwood floor had a waxy shine. Perry had the sudden urge to remove his shoes, take a running start and slide across the floor in his socks. But he didn't. There was a case to solve.

They continued past the kitchen and through the living room to a sliding glass door.

McKenzie unlocked it and slid the door along its tracks. The two stepped onto a large wooden deck with white wicker furniture. Bees buzzed near a flower garden planted along one side of the deck. Perfectly trimmed green grass covered the large backyard. Along the edge of the fence was an oak tree. A rusty metal ladder ran up the base of the tree to a treehouse about six feet off the ground.

"That's my clubhouse." She pointed to it with her finger. "My dad built it for me on my eighth birthday. I have a lockbox up there that I keep my baseball cards in. This morning when I went up there, the box had been broken into and all my cards were gone except for my Johnny Bench card."

Perry nodded. He opened his bag, took out the notebook and pen and wrote some notes. When he finished, he looked at McKenzie. "How come they didn't take the Johnny Bench card?"

"They did, but it must have fallen because I found it on the floor."

Perry looked at the wooden structure. The faded white paint needed a new coat. Access into the fort was through a hole cut out at the base of the treehouse. There didn't seem to be any windows. Perry was about to ask if the fort had electricity when a figure emerged from the treehouse and climbed down the ladder.

"Butch," McKenzie yelled. "What are you doing in my fort? You know no one's allowed unless I'm up there."

Butch's face turned red. "Sorry," he said. "I knocked on your door, and when nobody answered I just figured you were in the treehouse."

McKenzie nodded. "Did you hear someone stole my ... hey,

what do you have in your hands?"

Butch moved his hands behind his back. "None of your beeswax. That's what."

Normally no one took that sort of tone with McKenzie on the threat she would pummel them, but Butch was different. He was thirteen, two years older than McKenzie and several inches taller.

Perry put his notebook in his bag and stepped forward. "Can I see the cards?" he asked.

"Why should I? These are mine and anything McKenzie tells you is a lie."

Perry smiled. "Then you won't mind if I take a look at them."

Butch sighed. "Fine," and handed them to him.

"Those are my cards," McKenzie screamed. "You're the thief."

Perry didn't feel comfortable between these two bullies. All it would take was one false move, one wrong word, and he might be a witness or even a victim to World War III. He cleared his throat and looked at Butch.

"You say these are your cards. I need proof you aren't lying.

Can you do that?"

McKenzie stepped forward and snatched the cards out of Perry's hands. One of the cards fell to the ground. Butch picked it up.

"See this card,' he said, handing it to Perry. "It's Derek Jeter's rookie card. My dad bought it for me when I was four. That's when Derek Jeter played his first game as a New York Yankee."

Perry studied the card. On the front stood a player throwing a ball across the baseball diamond toward first base. Printed in white letters along the bottom of the card was the name Derek Jeter. Along the top was 1992 Draft Pick also printed in white.

Perry scratched his head. He had been hired to investigate a case. Solve a crime. Bring justice to the victim. But as he stared at the baseball card in his hand, he wondered if there had been a crime committed at all. Maybe these were Butch's cards and McKenzie wanted them for herself. He knew kids fought over all sorts of things that did not belong to them. McKenzie might have been lying all along.

As he handed the card back to Butch, something caught his eye. Something Butch had said proved the card could not be his. Perry smiled at him. "This is not your card and I can prove it."

Did you solve the case too? If not, turn to the next page to find out how Perry solved the case.

    Hint: Take another look at the title and subtitle of the chapter.

Butch told Perry his father bought him the card when he was four years old. The same year Derek Jeter started his rookie year. Butch is thirteen. He wouldn't have been born yet.

Chapter 10

Death at a Funeral

Detective Stacie Filmore dabbed her eyes with a tissue from the box on the pew. If only she'd had one more day with her older sister. Life was so unfair.

Stacie's husband, Josh, squeezed her hand and gave her a weak smile. His gesture was comforting, but the sadness remained.

She glanced around. The room was a gloomy one, functional but cold. But she figured most funeral homes were.

Then her gaze fell upon the casket. The thought of never talking to her sister again brought on another bout of nausea. This one caused bile to creep up the back of her throat. As a homicide detective, she'd been to countless crime scenes, seen more dead bodies than she cared to remember, but the death of her sister. She needed to get a breath of air. And fast.

Stacie stood, but then the room started to spin. Vertigo had bad timing. Josh reached out and grabbed her hand to keep her from falling.

"Are you okay?" he asked.

She closed her eyes trying to get a handle on the situation. Didn't seem to work. "I think I'm going to be sick."

Stacie opened her eyes. At least the room quit swirling, but the nausea never let up. Josh forged ahead, leading her by the hand. The large crowd that had assembled in the pews stared at her. *They must think I'm weak.*

Stacie pulled free from Josh and ran down the aisle. This was a race. The lady's restroom was locked. She knocked several times, but no one answered.

She tried the male restroom. A sigh of relief flooded through her when the doorknob turned. She made a beeline for the toilet.

After throwing up twice and dry heaving once, she stood and walked to the sink to rinse the horrible taste out of her mouth. Too bad she hadn't brought toothpaste or a toothbrush.

Stacie stared at herself in the mirror. Her eyeliner streaked a little down her cheeks. Her sister would've teased her about such things, which brought on a weak smile. Then Stacie laughed.

The door opened and Josh entered. "You feel better?"

"I'll be okay."

When they were back to their seats, the chaplain was talking about her sister. When the ceremony ended, people approached and gave their condolences.

A woman screamed in the foyer. Then another person yelled, "We need help."

A small crowd congregated around the lady's restroom.

"Is she dead?" someone asked.

Stacie approached and made her way inside the restroom. On the floor lay a woman in her mid-forties. Stacie checked for a pulse. Nothing.

A syringe stuck out of the dead woman's right arm. This appeared to be an accidental overdose. Still, the scene needed to be cleared.

After kicking everyone out, Stacie decided to spend a little time to take in the surroundings and note any clues for the arriving detectives. She had a funeral to attend.

The woman didn't appear to have any track marks on her arms.

Are you a recreational user?

The deceased wore a gold watch on her left wrist. The screen was cracked.

Did that happen when you fell?

She scanned the rest of the area. A pair of prescription glasses was on the back of the sink. The lenses were thick. This struck her as odd because she didn't know if the woman could see without them.

Then she noticed the back of the right earpiece of the glasses had been chewed. Stacie's mother had done the same thing for years, which drove her dad nuts.

She took in her surroundings one more time, because appearances are not always what they seem. She stared at the syringe in the right arm. The case needed to be investigated further because she believed the woman might have been murdered.

How did Stacie come to this conclusion?

Hint: Watch and prescription glasses.

The woman on the floor had a syringe in her right arm. She wore a gold watch on her right wrist and the right earpiece of prescription eyeglasses was chewed. Both indicate a right-handed person.

If the woman were right-handed, she would have stuck the syringe in her left arm.

Chapter 11

Case of the Stolen Headdress

The bus ride out to Camp Wiki-Wiki was the same as it had been the past three years as Perry Winkle looked out a dirt caked window. Trees lined the side of a bumpy road in dire need of new pavement as the kids sang songs along with the camp master, Ted Wilkens, and his staff, Carl Levinson, and Rocky Duggan. The three men loved to sing on the 2-hour bus ride as the kids sang along.

Normally, Perry loved the trip, but his mind was focused on his junior detective agency. He had seen more clients and solved more cases over the past few weeks than he had in six months. Business was booming and he didn't like the idea of having to close shop to spend a week at the camp.

What worried him even more was what McKenzie Callahan said as the bus pulled away from the curb of his house. "Don't worry about the crime rate increasing in the neighborhood because I'm opening up my own detective service." Then she gave a crooked grin, the one Perry knew all too well. It meant McKenzie was up to no good. Then she added, "I think I'll call it The Around the Clock Detective Service." She laughed. "Don't worry. I'm sure there's enough crime for us to share."

Perry didn't think she was serious, but if she did open a detective agency, she might bully his clients to hire her. Not only that, but he didn't think McKenzie had the brains to be cut out as a junior detective. Her specialty was committing crimes, not solving them.

The bus came to a stop. Dust from the dirt road floated in the air, causing Perry to sneeze.

"Okay," Mr. Wilkens yelled above the noisy kids. "Get your bags and exit the bus in an orderly fashion. Once everyone is in the cafeteria, we'll assign cabins."

Perry reached under the seat and grabbed his suitcase. Two more buses pulled alongside, and kids could be heard singing.

When he walked toward the cafeteria, the famed Indian Headdress worn by Chief Wiki-Wiki, for whom the camp was named rested in a locked glass enclosure. Chief Wiki-Wiki and his tribe were known for their remarkable tracking ability.

Inside the cafeteria, Perry sat with several other kids. Soon all the tables were full of children. Mr. Wilkens stood at the head table with the other tribal counselors and tapped a glass with a fork. A moment later, the room fell silent.

"My staff and I want to welcome you to Camp Wiki-Wiki," Wilkens said. "I would like to welcome two new tribal counselors, Mr. Miller and Mr. Taylor." Two men from his right stood and waved to the crowd.

"They come to us from our rival tribe, Chippi-Wawa."

Boos resonated from the crowd. The Chippi-Wawa's won most of the competitions each year. There were rumors they cheated in the events, but no one could ever prove it.

Wilkens raised a hand in the air. The noise lowered to a soft murmur. "I expect each of you to welcome our new counselors. Now if there's nothing else, your teepee assignments are listed on the wall to my left. After you get settled, you're free to go to the archery range, canoeing, or walk around the camp. But the cafeteria is off-limits until lunchtime. Now go out and have fun."

Perry was assigned to teepee three along with six other boys. The outside looked just like a teepee. A tall, cone-shaped tent, but instead of using buffalo skin, the teepee was made of canvass. He walked through the door and saw several of his bunkmates putting their things away.

Perry walked to an empty bunk bed and decided to take the bottom one. He didn't want to have to climb up and down, especially when he was tired. One year, he rolled off the top and chipped a tooth on the wooden floor.

"My name is William," a voice said behind him. Perry turned and saw a tall, lanky kid with glasses and short hair, combed perfectly to the side. He wore a navy-blue collared shirt and khaki shorts. He thought William dressed more for the yacht club than the great outdoors.

"I'm Perry Winkle."

They shook hands.

William tossed his suitcase on the top bunk and asked, "What are you going to do until lunchtime?"

"I'm thinking about going to the archery range. I want to beat our rivals this year."

"Are they any good?"

Perry nodded. "Chippi Wawa has won the competition the last five years."

William opened his suitcase and removed his clothes. "How many years have you been coming here?"

Perry put a copy of the latest issue of *The Old Time Mystery* and placed it under his pillow to read later. "This is my third year. How about you?"

"This is my first. I've never been to a camp like this before. I got lost trying to find my teepee. Had to get directions four times."

"Do you want to come with me and shoot some targets?"

"Sure. You're the first friend I've found here."

When they arrived at the archery range, there were about thirty other kids shooting round targets with arrows. Several staff members demonstrated how to use a bow and line up the arrow.

William tapped Perry on the shoulder. "I'll be right back. I have to use the restroom."

Perry thought about giving his new friend directions, but William had already darted down the trail. Perry stepped toward one of the staff members and picked up a bow and arrow.

"Do you need some archery lessons?"

"No, sir."

The sun bore down, and the heat rose over the next hour. Sweat dripped down Perry's forehead stinging his eyes. He used the back of his hand to wipe it away.

A loud horn startled him as he shot an arrow downrange. He missed the target and the shaft skirted across some grass before resting next to a tree stump.

"What's that noise?" a kid asked.

"We're being called back to the cafeteria," a staff member said.

In the three years Perry had been coming here, he'd only heard the horn once. Several kids had gotten food poisoning after eating potato salad brought in by one of the boys. He wondered what had happened now. Perry looked around but didn't see William. Maybe he got lost and now a search party was being formed.

When he got back to the cafeteria, he found William sitting at a table by himself. Perry sat next to him.

"What happened to you? You never came back."

William shrugged. "Something bad has happened."

One of the janitors ran to the head table and had a short conversation with camp master Wilkens. Mr. Wilkens's ears perked. Then he shot from his chair and banged a fork on the table to get everyone to be silent.

"First of all, I have some disturbing news. Burglars have broken into our camp this morning and stolen Chief Wiki-Wiki's headdress."

A murmur went around the cafeteria.

"Obviously, this is a serious matter and the police have been called. I suggest you all hand in any valuables to the staff. And always keep the doors to your teepees locked. If you see anything unusual or anyone you don't recognize on the campgrounds, report it to my staff or me immediately. Is that clear?"

Perry turned to William. "Did you see anyone suspicious while you were out?"

"Yes. After I left the archery range to find a restroom, I got lost and ended up back at the cafeteria. I saw two men breaking into the case and they took out the headdress. One of them was wearing sunglasses."

Perry took out his notepad and pencil. The *Old Time Mystery* stories always reiterated to be prepared because one never knew when a case might pop up.

William continued. "Then they turned back toward me. Maybe to make sure the coast was clear. I ducked behind some bushes so they couldn't see me. That's when I noticed their eyes."

"Their eyes?" Perry asked. "What about them?"

"One had green eyes, the other blue. I thought they saw me, but I froze trying not to let them know where I was."

"What happened next?"

"They took the headdress and ran down one of the trails. Just as I stood, I saw Bart Miller and Zack Taylor walk up."

"You mean the two new counselors from Chippi Wa-Wa?"

William nodded. "They noticed the case was broken and headdress missing. Then I heard a loud horn and now we're here."

Perry looked down at his notes. Maybe there was a clue to identify the thieves.

After reading his notes a second time he knew who stole the headdress.

Did you solve the case too? If not, turn to the next page to find out who stole the headdress.

William, Bart Miller, and Zach Taylor are the thieves.

William told Perry he needed to go to the restroom, but how could he have known where one was if he hadn't been to Camp Wiki-Wiki before. He told Perry he got lost just trying to find his teepee. He described one of the thieves as having blue eyes and the other green. He couldn't have seen the color of the person's eyes behind the sunglasses.

William also mentioned Bart Miller and Zach Taylor walked up shortly after the crime, but he couldn't have known their first names unless he knew them. They were introduced by camp master Wilkens as Mr. Miller and Mr. Taylor.

Chapter 12

Suicide or Homicide?

Detective Fin Roberts arrived at 1026 Stanton Road shortly after 1 p.m. The mailman had called to report a foul stench. Since the city was enduring one of the longest heat waves in recent years, he didn't put much stock in the postman's observation.

In Roberts's line of work, people often thought the worst of a situation, only to discover there had been a dead animal or a leaking sewage line. But the tip needed to be investigated, nonetheless.

The address turned out to be a trailer. Rust stains ran down the aluminum sides. The windows were caked in dirt and grime. He hoped the inside fared better. But if the outside looked this bad, the inside was probably much worse.

An elderly man and woman stood near a fence made of chicken wire that separated the two properties.

A mailman approached as he made his way toward the porch.

"Are you the detective?" the postman asked.

"I am. And are you the one who made the call?"

"Yes, sir. My name is Stanley Moore, but most people call me Rusty."

"Okay, Rusty. What can you tell me about the person or persons who reside here?"

"Her name is Tracy Black."

"And what made you call the police?"

Stanley scratched his scalp. "Well, her mail has been piling up and then there's the foul stench."

"Could she be out of town?"

Rusty shrugged. "It's possible, but the couple standing in the yard next door know her better than I do. They're Tom and Becky

Watson."

Roberts thanked him and walked to the Watsons. After quick introductions he learned they lived next to Tracy Black for the past three years.

"Could she be out of town," Roberts asked.

"I don't think so," Becky Watson said. She pointed to a well-used sedan. "That's her car."

"What can you tell me about her?"

Tom cleared his throat. "She used to be a flight instructor. Flying was her life. Her passion. But four years ago, she crashed a plane. One of her students died. Tracy suffered serious injuries which required a number of surgeries."

"Does she still fly?"

"No. The FAA revoked her license, and she was fired from her job."

"She currently employed?"

Becky nodded. "Odd jobs here and there, but nothing full-time."

"Thank you," Roberts said. "I may come back and ask more

questions."

The detective walked up the rickety steps. Several creaked so loud he thought they might break. Before he reached the front door, he caught a whiff of a scent with which he was all too familiar.

He tried the doorknob, but it was locked.

"There's a key under the mat," Becky said from across the yard.

The inside of the trailer was fairly clean. Much better than he gave credit for. The kitchen was free of dishes, the living room clear of trash except for a stack of overdue bills on the coffee table. Next to the bills was an empty bottle of pain pills. He read the prescription and noticed it had been filled three days ago.

He set the bottle down and made his way toward the foul smell. Each of the bedrooms along the way were clean. The bathroom didn't have any clutter. Tracy Black kept a tidy place.

When he opened the master bedroom in the back of the trailer, the rancid smell made his eyes water. The body of a decomposing woman lay on the bed. Flies swarmed her.

Then he noticed the clutter in the room. A chair had been

knocked on its side. The dresser drawers had been pulled out and clothes littered the floor.

He walked to the vanity in a corner where a jewelry box had been opened. There were several gold earrings, necklaces and a pearl necklace that appeared genuine.

Roberts searched the room to make sure he hadn't missed any evidence. He would need to get a crime scene team out here to dust for fingerprints, but he was sure this was a suicide and not a murder.

Why does Detective Fin Roberts believe this is a suicide?

His first clue is the front door was locked. If someone ransacked the house after killing Tracy Black, they probably wouldn't lock the door behind them.

The second clue is the empty pain prescription bottle. It had been filled three days earlier. There should be more pills.

The final clue was the bedroom. Although it appeared as though someone rummaged through the room, nothing was taken. No thief would leave behind valuable jewelry.

Fin Roberts believes Tracy Black committed suicide but wanted to make it appear as though she'd been murdered. He didn't know if she did this because she was so far in debt, she was in too much pain, or the fact the FAA took away her pilot license.

Chapter 13

The Story

Ted Chaires, along with a group of other boys gathered around the campfire. They'd been camping the past three nights. The air was crisp and 2019 was coming to an end.

Mr. Cooper, a twenty-eight-year-old single dad, handed out marshmallows. Some of the other kids had chocolate and graham crackers to make s'mores, but Ted liked to roast his marshmallows by themselves.

"Okay, boys," Mr. Cooper said. "I'm going to tell you a spooky story that's true."

"What's it about?" Craig Stone asked.

"It's a ghost story."

Craig's eyes widened. "I hope it's not too scary."

"Quit being a baby," Craig's older brother, Doyle, said. "There's no such thing as ghosts."

Ted wasn't sure the boy was right. He'd always believed ghosts were real although he'd never actually seen one.

"It all started in my grandfather's house," Mr. Cooper began. "One evening during early spring in the nineteenth century, my grandfather, who was a farmer and had just finished working the crops. When he walked into the house, he heard an eerie sound, but when he went to investigate, he couldn't find where the noise came from, so my grandpa chalked it up as the wind.

The next day he heard the same noise. He asked my grandma, Thelma, if she'd heard the sound. She told him it was the wind. He didn't think so but couldn't prove otherwise.

On the third day, he went to the basement. A ghostly figure

emerged with an axe and chased grandpa through the house. Turns out the figure was *his* grandfather who was murdered with an axe."

"What happened to the ghost?" Ted heard someone ask.

"He continues to chase anyone who enters the house."

"And you've seen him?" Craig asked.

"No."

"Then how can you believe the story?" Doyle asked.

Mr. Cooper stood, wielding an axe. "Because I am the ghost."

Several kids screamed. Craig ran into the woods. Doyle chased after him.

Mr. Cooper laughed.

A moment later, Craig and Doyle returned.

"Is that story real?" Craig asked.

"Sure is," Mr. Cooper said. "Except for the part about me being the ghost."

Ted smiled. "Actually, none of it is real."

Why did Ted think the story wasn't real?

Hint: Nineteenth Century

James Glass

Mr. Cooper said the story took place in the Spring of the nineteenth century. His grandfather wouldn't have been born yet, because the nineteenth century was during the 1800s.

Chapter 14

Running Man

Caleb Johnson checked to make sure the laces on his Nikes were tied in double knots. The last time he competed in a local run, his shoes had come untied. The five seconds needed to stop and lace them had cost him the win. The loss crushed him, and he promised he wouldn't make the same mistake twice.

The Bridge to Bridge 15-kilometer run was one of the biggest in the city. Several thousand runners had signed up for the 9.3-mile race. The grand prize was a thousand dollars.

Spectators lined both sides of Main Street. They were rooting for their friends and loved ones.

Caleb moved toward the starting line, adrenaline coursing through him. His rival, Rick Ayers stood to his left. The man had beat him by three seconds' last time. Today would be different. This time, Caleb knew he'd be the one crossing the finish line first.

Another runner moved to his left. The tall, thin man wore shiny new Reeboks. The bright red shoes appeared to glow in the sunlight.

"Runners," Mayor Fred Thompson said from a podium to the front and left of the starting line. The mayor raised a starter pistol in the air. "Get set. Go!" and fired the pistol. The bang resonated in the air.

The large digital clock overhead began to count. The race had officially started.

About twenty runners darted in front of Caleb, but he knew many of them would fall behind after time because their pace was too fast to maintain over the entire distance. He lost track of the man in the red shoes as they passed by the port-o-potties. Rick Ayers however, maintained the same steady pace as Caleb.

As the two crossed the first bridge at mile-marker four, Caleb had moved into first place. Rick had fallen into second, about twenty yards behind.

Gray clouds moved overhead, threatening to dump rain as the two runners crossed the second bridge at mile-marker six.

A headwind picked up and Caleb slowed his pace ever so slightly. He didn't want to overextend his energy reserves.

At mile seven, the course led the runners onto an unpaved street. The rain finally came. The steady raindrops quickly turned into a torrential downpour creating massive mud puddles along the dirt road. Caleb still maintained the lead.

He passed by mile marker eight which turned back onto Main Street. The race started and ended at the same place. Two minutes later he saw the finish line. He knew victory was his until he saw one of the doors to the port-a-potties open and the man in the red shoes sprinted a hundred yards ahead of Caleb, crossing the finish line first.

How had the man passed him, and he never saw him? He

knew the rain came down hard, limiting his vision, but he figured he would still have seen someone pass him. This hadn't made sense.

Disappointment turned into anger as Caleb crossed the finish line. Thirty-five seconds later, his rival followed suit.

"Congratulations," Rick said, patting Caleb on the shoulder.

"Thanks, but I didn't win."

Rick stared at him. "What do you mean? It was you and me for the last three miles."

Caleb pointed to the man being congratulated by a small crowd. "The guy over there wearing the shiny red shoes beat me."

"How?"

"I don't know. I never saw him until I came out of the dirt road. Then he popped out of the port-a-potty and beat me to the finish line by about a hundred yards."

"Something doesn't add up. I never saw him either," Rick said. "I think we have a cheater."

"I thought the same thing, but I can't prove he cheated."

The crowd around the winner dispersed and the man approached Rick and Caleb. "Nice race guys. I didn't know if I'd win or not, but you guys really made it a challenge."

The man bent down and tied one of his running shoes. Caleb sighed then hung his head in utter defeat. He couldn't believe this man won. As the man tied his shiny, red Reebok's Caleb tried to figure out how the man cheated.

"Congratulations to all the participants," Mayor Thompson began. He stood at the podium, a large smile on his face. "I'd like to give a special thank you to this year's winner, Parker Phillips."

The crowd applauded, but Caleb still stewed over the defeat. As Parker made his way to receive his trophy, Caleb finally realized Parker cheated. The man had made a big mistake. One he couldn't account for during the race.

Did you find the mistake?

Hint: Parker Phillips running shoes.

When Parker Phillips tied his shoes after the race, they were still shiny. If he'd ran down the dirt road, his shoes would have mud on them.

Parker Phillips cheated by staying in the port-a-potty, which prevented his shoes from getting muddy.

Chapter 15

Death of a Salesman

Stanley Goodman always liked the idea of being the best vacuum cleaner salesman for all of Baker County. His good looks and easy demeanor always got him in the front door of any household. The key to the sale had always been his pitch. "If I can't clean your carpets in thirty minutes or less, I'll give you a free vacuum cleaner."

No matter how many times he pitched this, everyone took him up on the challenge. The reason for his success had been dependent on knowing the layout of the house before he arrived. To do this, he would find a way to enter the home beforehand.

Most families worked during the day, so he would wait for them to leave before entering through the front door. It was amazing to him how many people still left their homes unlocked during the day.

Once he gained access, he would map out each room and know how long it would take to ensure his victory. The only downfall was when the occupants owned a dog. One time he'd been bitten in the derriere by a Doberman and needed several stitches. On another occasion, the residence had a rather large pig and the animal walked across his foot, breaking one of Stanley's toes. Both incidents were setbacks, but he always managed to come back with a grin and a sale.

That is up until his untimely death at 2119 Willowick Circle. Stanley had been found face down in a pool of blood in the kitchen floor.

On the kitchen table were two glasses of tea and a plate of chocolate chip cookies.

The owner of the home, Donna Montgomery stated to the

police, Stanley had tried to sell her a vacuum cleaner. After she rejected his offer to clean her carpets in thirty minutes or less, he tried to seduce her. When she still refused, he forced himself in the house anyway. Ms. Montgomery would later state to the police she feared for her life and ran from him, but he gave chase. She felt compelled to defend herself, by knocking him over the head with a brass candlestick.

The medical examiner later confirmed that Stanley died of blunt force trauma to the back of his skull and that his injuries were consistent with the marks left by the candlestick.

However, after a more thorough investigation, the detectives were able to reconstruct the events that led to Stanley's demise and were confident his death was a homicide and not self-defense.

Turn the page to find out why the detectives suspected Donna Montgomery of killing Stanley Goodman.

Hint: Head wound.

Donna Montgomery stated she ran from Stanley because she feared for her life. She grabbed a candlestick and struck him in the head. The only problem with this scenario is if she were running away from him and she swung the candlestick, she couldn't have hit him in the back of the head.

There was also two cups of tea and a plate of cookies on the kitchen table which led the detectives to believe Stanley was struck in the back of the head while he sat at the table.

Chapter 16

The Phone Call

Detective Frank Knox walked through the front door of his house at 9:15 p.m.

Exhausted, this had been one of the longest days of his career. Thanksgiving was usually an easy day to earn time-and-a-half and not worry about too much trouble. He'd planned his day around the football games. But fate had intervened. Three homicide investigations in one day must've been a new record.

All he wanted to do now was veg out in front of the TV and drink a few beers.

Frank grabbed a brewski from the fridge, popped the top and took a long pull. The cold bit the back of his throat. He plopped down in his well-worn recliner and flipped the television on.

The New Orleans Saints were driving the ball down the field. They were leading the Atlanta Falcons 21-to-3 in the third quarter. At least his day hadn't been a total loss. He'd take in some football after all.

The house phone interrupted his relaxation time. When he got up to get another cold one, he'd take the phone off the hook. He took another long pull of his beer.

The answering machine clicked on. "Detective Knox, this is Jeffrey Devers."

Frank almost choked as he swallowed. Jeffrey Devers was on trial for seven murders. The man hacked his victims with a machete. Their remains were found in shallow graves at an abandoned park.

The trial was being covered by Court TV and every news channel wanted a piece of the sensational story. Even Hollywood wanted in on the action. Rumor was a big-name director was penned to turn the tragedy into a box office hit.

Somehow Devers' attorney managed to pull the first of many miracles during the trial by convincing the judge his client deserved to be out on bond.

The judge thought forty million would keep the man incarcerated, but miraculously Devers produced the ten percent.

Frank snagged the phone. "What do you want, scumbag?"

"I see we're in a mood this evening, Detective. Must be the full moon. All the police shows say the crazy stuff happens on a full moon. Is that true?"

Frank didn't want to get into a debate with this asshole, but the man was right. The full moon did seem to cause more havoc around the city than any other night. Or at least that had been his experience.

"Why did you call me? I'm sure your lawyers would have advised against it."

"Ah, lawyers. The bane of my existence. Want to hear a joke?"

Frank squeezed the phone. He didn't have time for games.

Instead, he wanted to reach through the phone and choke the life out of Devers.

"Come on detective. At least give me the common courtesy and at least play along."

"All right, I'll play, but I want to make sure you understand your rights."

"There's no need to bring up Miranda. Not that anyone cares."

"Piss off. And don't call here again. Ever."

"Fine, fine. Has anyone ever told you that you're a pain in the ass?"

After Frank read him his rights, Devers asked, "What do you call a hundred lawyers at the bottom of the ocean?"

"A head start."

"You're no fun. You're such a buzz kill."

Frank ignored his remark. "Why did you call?"

"Can't a man gab it up with an old friend?"

"We're not friends, Devers. So, get to the point." He knew the serial killer was too smart to fall for the common interrogation tricks, so he figured his gruffness might do the trick for now.

"Okay, then tell me why I killed those people. After all, you're a hotshot detective, aren't you?"

"Am I?"

"You go first," Devers said.

"You enjoy seeing your victims beg for their lives as you kill them in the most sadistic way possible."

"Why would you call me sadistic?"

"So, you don't deny killing them?"

"I didn't say that."

"Now who's being the party pooper."

"Say I did kill them. Why would you call me sadistic?"

"Because you hacked them up with a hatchet."

"Not bad, detective. But I wouldn't consider the act sadistic."

"You're right, but you hacked them to pieces while they were still alive and that makes you sadistic."

"I'm impressed. You're a modern Sherlock Holmes. Does that make me your Moriarty?"

Frank didn't see himself as Holmes and this guy certainly wasn't Moriarty. But he decided to play along.

"You don't get off that easy, Devers. Tell me something only the killer would know."

"They did scream. And those screams were music to my ears."

This was good, but Frank needed more to bury this guy. A piece of evidence or a confession his lawyers couldn't destroy on cross-examination. "How did you select your victims?"

"I'll never tell."

"Guess you really aren't my Moriarty after all."

"You must think I'm an idiot."

"Well, every village has one."

Devers laughed. "Touché. But why should I tell you how I found them?"

"Call me old fashioned. I like to open doors for women, pay for dinner on a date, and never kiss and tell."

"You're a straight shooter. Boring, but a straight shooter."

"We all have our weaknesses."

"Pray tell, detective."

"Tell me how you selected your victims, and I will."

Devers sighed on the other end. "Fine. They were all born on

February 29th. Happy?"

He was. Only the age had been leaked to the media, but not their birthdays. A shot of adrenaline coursed through him.

"Not that any of this matters, Detective. No one will ever hear my confession. It's a moot point. Not to mention, it's your word against mine. Add to the fact I'm calling you from a throw-away phone. Guess this does make me the smarter man. Until next time Sherlock."

Devers hung up, leaving Frank to consider the last statement. The man was right. No one would ever hear his confession.

Then Frank realized Devers made a mistake. One that could be used in court. Did you find the mistake?

Frank Knox would be able to use the confession because it was recorded on his answering machine.

The only sticking point would be to get a professional to verify the voice on the recording as belonging to Jeffrey Devers.

Chapter 17

The Hitchhiker

Josh Morgan, a traveling salesman, was driving along at a steady clip along Highway 89. He usually enjoyed traveling along the Interstates because the speed limit allowed him to get to his destinations quickly.

Today had been a momentous day. His client, a man with deep pockets signed a huge contract that would guarantee Josh a five-figure bonus at the end of the year. His stomach gurgled. He glanced at the clock on the dashboard. He'd been on the road for over three hours.

His mood carried him past lunch. An early dinner sounded like a nice treat. Maybe he could find a diner soon.

Up ahead he noticed a hitchhiker. Not one to normally pick up strangers, he found himself wanting to do a good deed. Josh pulled along the shoulder and lowered the window. He wanted to see if the man had really bad body odor. If so, he'd drive on, leaving the stranger behind.

"Where are you headed?" Josh asked.

The hitchhiker, a man of average height and build, wearing a wrinkled shirt and faded jeans leaned into the window. "Anywhere but here."

Josh detected a faint scent of cologne. He smiled at the stranger. "I just happen to be headed anywhere but here. Hop on in."

The man opened the door and sat in the passenger seat, placing his backpack on the floorboard.

Josh found it odd the man's clothes were clean. He figured they'd be caked in dirt, but then again, he might be reading into it.

"I'm Josh."

"Matt."

"How long have you been traveling on the roads?"

"On and off again for about nine months."

"Seeing the country?"

"Something like that."

Josh pulled the car back onto the road. "I'm hungry. You know any good diners in the area?"

Matt nodded. "There's one about five miles ahead. Turn right onto Sycamore Avenue and then take the second left, which is Byron Street."

"Great. Care to join me?"

"I don't have any money."

"That's okay. My treat." Josh didn't know why he was being so generous with the guy. Maybe it was the salesman in him. His motto had always been, 'Keep them talking.' But he wasn't trying to make a sale here.

"Are you sure?" Matt asked.

"Absolutely."

An awkward silence filled the car, so Josh turned the radio on.

"This is a news update," the jockey said. "Police are on the lookout for an unidentified man who robbed a local gas station. He is believed to be—"

"Sorry," Matt said changing the station. "Can we listen to music?"

"I guess."

After searching through several stations playing, a variety of music, they settled on a country station.

Matt pointed. "Turn here."

Josh turned right. He passed a post office with a small barbershop next door. A jewelry store was across the street. Next to the store was a coffee shop.

"Take the next left," Matt said.

He did. Becky's All-American Diner came into view. He pulled into the parking lot and found a place near the front. Even at two, business seemed to be good.

They walked inside and waited for the hostess. The aroma of burgers, fires, steaks, and a combination of various foods made Josh's mouth water.

A moment later they were seated at a booth. The server

approached, took their orders, and disappeared into the kitchen.

"You said you've been traveling for about nine months." Josh said. "Been through any interesting cities?"

"Here and there, but nothing has kept my interest long enough to stay in any one place."

Josh nodded as if he understood but really didn't. His job took him all over the country and he always found each city interesting in its own way. Whether they had the best chocolate malt, an old drive-in theatre, or beautiful beaches.

The server returned with flapjacks and an omelet for Josh. Matt opted for the burger and fries.

They both ate in silence a while.

"How long have you been in town?" Josh asked.

Matt shook his head. "Not long. I was just passing through when you happened by."

"Any idea where you want to go next?"

"Anywhere but here."

Josh sipped some coffee, contemplating his next move. Three things led him to believe Matt might be the man the police were looking for.

How did Josh come to this conclusion? Did you uncover the two things?

Hint: Diner

When Josh picked up Matt on the side of the road, the man's clothes were wrinkled but didn't smell. If the man had been traveling for nine months his clothes wouldn't be clean. Matt did this to draw suspicion away from him.

The second thing was the cologne. He didn't know for sure, but why would a hitchhiker wear cologne.

The final reason was Matt stated he was only passing though the town. If this were true, how could he know where the diner was? He provided specific directions.

Chapter 18

Brothers

Detective Arlin Eubanks stood in the living room where a husband named Jonathan Baker hung himself. Baker was wearing an immaculate gray suit. But his shoes were well-worn. Eubanks wondered if the shoes carried any significance in the man's life.

Or maybe they were used to send a message to his wife, who apparently left him for another woman. He supposed the significance if there was one didn't really matter.

Two weeks before offing himself, the now deceased husband

amended his will so his mother would inherit the bulk of his estate.

Baker had placed the new will next to the suicide note. The note had only six words but spoke volumes. *You get nothing, you cheating bitch!*

Detective Eubanks never understood marriage. Over the span of his thirty-five years on this earth, he'd avoided settling down. The detective had worked some strange cases in the past, but this one only reinforced his decision to remain single.

There were nights he wished for companionship but not enough for a committed relationship. He'd become an avowed bachelor.

His cell buzzed. He answered on the second ring.

"What's up, Lieutenant?"

"You done there?"

"Yeah."

"Good, because I've got another possible suicide at ... hold on I've got the address ... here it is 1711 Park Place."

"Who's the victim?"

Eubanks heard the lieutenant shuffle some papers. "A Walter

Hayes?"

"Who called it in, El-tee"?

"His brother, William."

Twenty minutes later, Eubanks arrived at 1711 Park Place. The ranch-style home was nestled in between two others, all three about the same size.

A large van took up most of the driveway, so he pulled the cruiser along the curb and parked behind a patrol vehicle and an ambulance.

A heavyset man, probably three hundred fifty pounds sat in a wheelchair on the landing outside the front door as two paramedics attended to him. A patrolman stood at the entrance to the front door.

Eubanks gestured for the officer to meet him at the bottom of the handicapped ramp leading to the front porch.

"What happened?"

The officer, whose nametag read *Johnson*, said, "When I arrived on scene I walked into the house where I discovered the body of Walter Hayes. He'd apparently blew his brains out, courtesy of a 9-millimeter."

"Do you suspect foul play?"

Johnson shrugged. "Doesn't appear to be, but you're the detective."

Eubanks pointed toward the man in the wheelchair. "He here when you arrived?"

"He was."

"He give a statement yet?"

"Only that he found the body."

"Anything else you'd like to add?"

Johnson shook his head.

Eubanks thanked him and made his way up the handicapped ramp leading to the porch. The paramedics were packing their gear.

"Is he okay?" Eubanks asked one of the paramedics.

"His blood pressure is a little high, but that's expected under the circumstances."

Eubanks nodded. "I'm sorry for your loss, Mr. Hayes." Hayes wore a pullover shirt, jeans, and a pair of well-worn tennis shoes.

"Thank you."

"Can I ask you some questions?"

"Sure. But please call me William." William extended his hand, and they shook. Eubanks didn't squeeze hard because the man had incredibly soft hands.

"Okay, William. Do you know why your brother would kill himself?"

"My brother has been under a lot of pressure. His house was in foreclosure and he'd been out of work for more than a month."

"So, this is your house?"

"It is. I was letting him stay until he could get back on his feet again."

"How long had he been living with you?"

William's eyes averted to the ground. "About two weeks."

"Did he have a wife or kids? Any next of kin?"

"No. Walter never did have much luck with the opposite sex."

"And did you witness the suicide?"

"Did I witness the suicide? No."

"But you found your brother, correct? You called 9-1-1?"

"Yes, on both."

"Can you elaborate?"

William cleared his throat. "A noise awakened me. At first, I thought the sound came from the television. But then I decided to go check. That's when I found my brother on the living room floor."

Eubanks pushed William through the front door. "May I ask how long you've been in a wheelchair?"

"Five years."

They moved down the hallway. Large windows let in the sunlight. Expensive furniture filled the living room. A fireplace took up a far wall. In the middle of the room lay the body of the deceased. The man was face up with a surprised expression on his face. Walter did indeed have a pistol in his right hand as Officer Johnson had indicated. A 9mm Beretta.

Upon closer observation, Eubanks noticed calluses on both hands. This reminded him of a former partner who was shot in the line of duty. His partner ended up in a wheelchair and developed calluses from competing in the weekly basketball games with other handicapped men.

He wondered if Walter's powerful hands were the reason he'd never let go of the gun after shooting himself.

"Did your brother leave a suicide note?"

"I didn't see one."

"Which room was he staying?"

William pointed down the hall. "Third door on the right."

When Eubanks entered the room, several suitcases were on the bed. He opened each one which were packed with an assortment of clothing, pictures, shoes, and various other items. He still didn't find a suicide note from the victim and he believed he knew why. This was a murder.

What lead Detective Eubanks to believe this to be a murder instead a suicide?

Hint: Handshake

When Detective Eubanks shook William Hayes hand, he noticed the man's skin was incredibly soft. If William had been in a wheelchair the past five years, he would have developed calluses like his former partner had.

William also showed signs of deception when asked basic questions. Indicators of someone lying are repeating the question they've been asked. This allows them time to formulate an answer. Throat clearing and averting their eyes are also indicators of deception.

William also wore a pair of well-worn shoes. Why would they be worn if he couldn't walk.

Finally, William stated his brother had been living there for two weeks, yet none of the suitcases had been unpacked.

Eubanks believes William is Walter and he killed his brother in a fit of rage because he was told he couldn't stay there. Instead of moving out, he decided to take his brother's identity and live there permanently.

Chapter 19

The Juror

On the third straight day of the Parker Phillips murderer trial, Judy Blume's eyeglasses fogged over as entered the warm building of the courthouse. It had been a harsh winter with temperatures hovering just above zero for the past six weeks, and the windchill didn't help matters.

She never thought she'd be selected for jury duty, much less a high-profile murder. The defendant, Cotton Franks was accused of murdering socialite, Parker Phillips. The trial began a year to the date of his murder.

As a crime writer, she figured Phillip's attorney would have used one of his peremptory challenges to remove her. After all, she'd always heard the defense didn't like cops, lawyers, or someone who doesn't seem sympathetic toward crimes their client may have committed.

Her family and friends told her she'd been selected because of her calming demeanor and keen eye for the details. She halfhearted believed this because as a writer she always searched for truth, not book sales.

By the time she entered the jury box and court started, her body quit shivering. The winters over the past several years seemed to get worse, but maybe she was exaggerating.

Most of her days were spent indoors, behind a computer writing her latest story or conducting research. On the rare occasion she took a break, she enjoyed watching classic television mystery shows like Perry Mason, Matlock, and her favorite—Murder She Wrote.

After the judge entered, took his seat behind the bench, the prosecutor, Dan Fouts, called his star witness. Well, the only witness wo claimed to see the murder take place.

Slade Phillips, the victim's only son and sole heir to the family fortune took the stand. After the bailiff swore him in, Fouts asked, "Mr. Phillips, what did you witness on the night of October 31st of last year?"

"I drove to father's house to ask about a loan for a new venture I was heading up."

"What time did you arrive?"

"Shortly after 7 pm."

"And what did you notice?"

Slade adjusted his glasses. Then he turned toward the jury. "I saw a man standing over my father with a bloody knife in his hand."

"Was your father dead?"

"Objection," the defense lawyer, Todd James said. "Calls for speculation."

The judge nodded. "Sustained."

Fouts asked, "Where did you see your father, Parker Phillips?"

"On the living room floor."

"Did you see blood?"

"Yes. Lots of it."

"Do you see the person who was holding the knife in the courtroom today?"

Slade pointed toward the defendant.

Fouts stood, "Let the record show the witness identified Cotton Franks."

The judge informed the court stenographer.

Fouts sat in his seat. "We have no further questions of the witness."

"The judge nodded and asked, "Does defense wish to cross-examine the witness?"

"We do your Honor." Todd James stood. "What was the weather like on the day you arrived at your daddy's house?"

"Cold."

"How cold?"

"I'm not a weatherman, but it was probably like today."

"Very well. And when you entered the house, did you see my

client right away?"

"I did."

"What color clothes was he wearing?"

"I don't recall."

"So, you don't have any idea, what he wore he supposedly stabbed your daddy to death?"

"Asked and answered," Fouts said."

"Sustained, the judge said. "Move along."

James nodded. "What were you going to see your father for?"

Slade adjusted his spectacles. "I was starting a new Venture."

"Venture and in a business?"

"Yes."

"And you needed money for a down payment?"

"Yes?"

"How much?"

"Three hundred thousand?"

"How many times has your daddy given you money for various ventures over the years?"

"A dozen."

"How many of these are still in business?"

Slade lowered his head. "None."

James opened a manilla folder and removed a sheet of paper. "Did you know your daddy removed you from his will?"

Fouts stood. "Your, Honor, what does this line of questioning have to do with the testimony?"

"Goes to motive," James said before the judge could respond.

Fouts countered, "Slade Phillips is not on trial for murder."

The judge nodded. "I agree. You're mucking up my trial with a red herring and I won't allow it. Now either move on or cut the witness loose."

But Judy realized there was no red herring. She knew Slade Phillips lied and she could prove it.

How did Judy know Slade Phillips lied on the stand?

When Judy entered the courthouse the weather outside was very cold and the temperature inside was warm causing her glasses to fog over.

Slade Phillips said the weather was very cold on the day his father was murdered. Slade claimed he saw Phillip Parker standing over his father's dead body immediately after entering the house. But like Judy, his glasses would have fogged over as well.

Chapter 20

The Case of Mistaken Identity

Perry sat in his favorite chair at the office, counting the money he'd made as the sole proprietor of the Pleasantville Junior Detective Agency. The drawer in his desk, his makeshift bank couldn't hold any more money. He needed to open an account at a bank.

He counted one-hundred-eighty-one dollars in five's and one-dollar bills. He grabbed the mason jar and tipped it over letting the quarters, dimes, and nickels scatter across the desk. It took him ten minutes to count and stack the coins in three separate piles. The piles made up 40 quarters, 30 dimes and 20 nickels.

He collected all the money and decided if he needed to open a bank account, he would need some protection from thieves. But who could he trust? His mom was busy making cookies and brownies for a bake sale for a charity he couldn't remember. His dad was at work at the One Stop Shop. If he wanted to open a bank account, he would need to hire someone to protect him and his money. But who?

Then a thought popped in his head. McKenzie Callahan. Although she was the neighborhood bully, he figured if he paid her for protection, she would keep him and his money safe. After all, who would dare rob McKenzie? She would give them a knuckle sandwich.

Perry stared at his money and weighed his options. Wait to open an account on another day with the possibility of being robbed. Or hire McKenzie. Thoughts swirled in his head as he contemplated his next move. Hiring McKenzie could be risky but being robbed would be worse.

He grabbed his crime scene kit and emptied the contents into the top drawer of the desk. Next, he scooped the money into the bag and decided to hire McKenzie.

Perry hopped on his bike and raced to McKenzie's house. He needed to get there before any robbers knew of his plans.

McKenzie opened the door. "What do you want pip squeak?"

Perry swallowed hard. He wondered if he'd made the right decision to come here. She could easily pummel him on the porch and take his money.

She growled. "Well, are you going to just stand there, or did you want something?"

Perry clutched the bag to his chest. His heart raced and he could hear the pounding in his ears. He wondered if she heard it too. Perry took a deep breath. "I want to hire you?"

"What for?"

"I want to open a bank account and I need some security to make sure I don't get robbed before I get there."

She gave a crooked grin. "How much money do you have?"

"That's none of your concern." Perry couldn't believe he just told her that. He decided to be brave. "But I will gladly pay you five dollars to get me to the bank without getting robbed."

"Make it ten and you got a deal."

Perry sighed. "Okay."

It seemed his plan to hire the neighborhood bully might pay off. They still had to make it to the bank, but he felt safer knowing McKenzie would be there to thwart any would be robbers.

They got on their bikes and headed toward the Pleasantville Bank.

Perry looked for any hiding places where someone could jump out and take his money. There were plenty of alleys as they rode their bikes down Main Street. A big dumpster sat near the corner of Baker Lane. As they turned down Market Street, no big thugs jumped out. But there was a boy of about Perry's age sitting on the sidewalk crying, his bike lying on the ground next to him.

"Don't stop," McKenzie said pedaling past the boy. "It might be a trap to steal your money."

Perry could see the whites of the boy's eyes when he looked up at him. He squeezed the brakes on his handlebars and stopped next the kid.

"What happened?"

Just then, another boy appeared from around the corner. He was bigger than McKenzie. Next to him was a police officer. The big kid pointed at McKenzie. "That's the one who stole our money."

"Stop!" the officer said to McKenzie. Her bike skidded on the sidewalk, leaving a curved trail the size of a black snake as she stepped on the brakes.

The police officer gestured with his hand. "Get back here."

"Okay, what's this about you taking this boy's money?"

McKenzie rolled her eyes at Perry and whispered, "I told you not to stop."

"The money is mine," Perry said. "We were on our way to the Pleasantville Bank."

"That's a lie," the kid on the ground cried out. He stood and walked to the officer. He shook the policeman's hand. "Thank goodness you arrived when you did. These two came out of nowhere and forced me off the road. My bike hit the curb of the sidewalk and I crashed. I've been crying because I scraped my hands."

The man stared at McKenzie. "You need to give the money back, or I will have to arrest you for stealing."

"We didn't do it," she insisted. "These two are lying, officer."

"Can you prove it?"

Her eyes stared at the sidewalk. "No sir."

Perry gave a crooked grin. "I can."

Did you figure out how Perry could prove to the Police Officer the boys lied? If not, turn to the next page to find out.

The boy sitting on the ground told the police officer Perry and McKenzie ran him off the road and he crashed onto the sidewalk scraping his hands. If the boy scraped his hands, he wouldn't have shaken hands with the police officer.

In addition, the boy stated he'd been crying, yet when Perry saw him, his eyes were white. If he'd been crying, his eyes would be red.

Chapter 21

Death of Betty Jo Davis

Detective Debbie Matthews walked through the front door to her house, ready to take a long bath before slipping into her pajamas. Sleep had been a forgone conclusion over the past several days due to the heavy caseloads. Murder never seemed to take a day off.

She drew a bath, poured in Epsom salts, and stepped into the tub. With a cry of relief, she inhaled the saline vapor.

The salt penetrated her nostrils as beads of sweat formed on her brow. The tension that built up over the past several days began to float away.

Her cell buzzed, bringing Debbie out of her tranquility.

She decided to let it go to voicemail.

The mobile chirped. A text. Debbie tried to ignore the intrusion, but her mind wouldn't let her. She glanced at the screen.

187

"Well, at least I'm still alive, which was more than I can say about that poor soul."

After getting dressed and feeling this day would bleed over until tomorrow, Debbie walked into the night and hopped into her unmarked cruiser.

Twenty minutes later she arrived at the crime scene, which was a large home in an upscale neighborhood.

A patrolman lifted the crime scene tape and Debbie ducked under. When she reached the front door, her boss, Captain Frank Smiley approached.

"Who's the victim?" Debbie asked.

"Senator Maxwell Davis and his wife Betty Jo. Appears to be a murder-suicide."

Debbie started to walk when Frank tugged at her shoulder. "I need to know if this is a murder-suicide."

She gave him a sideways glance. "What are you not telling me?"

Frank chewed his bottom lip. "The senator has been under investigation for embezzlement. He's been under a lot of pressure by the media and the FBI. I don't want to cloud your judgment, but something doesn't feel right about this one." He shook his head. "Call it a hunch."

Debbie wondered why he would tell her this. The man had been a detective for years before moving up the ladder. Although the man hadn't worked a homicide in over a decade, she didn't think he missed much. But apparently, he'd called her in because he wasn't sure about something. And she was determined to find out what.

He led her through the large house and upstairs to a spacious master bedroom. On the four-poster bed was the body of Betty Jo Davis. The victim lay on her back, arms spread eagle. She'd been wearing a white nightgown.

There was a broken vase on the floor next to the end table.

The husband, Maxwell, sat with his back against the wall, his head slumped forward. A .38 pistol was next to his right hand. So far, everything appeared to swing toward murder-suicide.

"Give me the details."

Franks pointed at the bed. "The victim's hands were restrained with handcuffs, each wrist shackled to one of the wooden posts of the headboard. There were heavy welts and marks around her neck indicative of strangulation. Other than her neck, she didn't appear to have any other marks or bruises on her body, including her wrists."

Franks turned and moved toward the second body.

"The senator ate his gun. He has an entry wound under his chin and massive damage along the top of the skull from the exit wound. He also has bruising along his temple. Possibly from falling to the floor after shooting himself.

"Both appear to be consistent with self-inflicted harm. His right hand also tested positive for gunshot residue."

"What about the vase?" Debbie asked.

"I'm thinking the senator hit his head on the end table after shooting himself causing the vase to fall and shatter. Or possibly the wife may have been able to struggle while he secured her with the handcuffs. Either would account for the vase being broken.

Frank scratched his head. "But something doesn't feel right. Like the scene's been staged. Plus, we haven't found a suicide note."

Debbie wasn't sure why Frank suspected foul play. Everything here appeared as a murder-suicide. And he'd been to enough scenes to know not everyone who killed themselves left a note.

She studied the scene one more time trying to see what appeared out of place. Then she understood why his gut told him something was wrong. And she thought she knew why. Three things at the scene pointed to a third person. The one who murdered Maxwell and Betty Jo Davis.

Do you know what three things Debbie found?

Hint: Ligature marks, temple, and location of Mr. Maxwell's body.

The victim, Betty Jo Davis had ligature marks around her neck indication she had been strangled. But there were no marks on her wrists from the handcuffs, which would have been there because she would have struggled to get free. This meant someone put them on after they killed her.

Maxwell had a bruise along his temple, which indicated someone knocked him unconscious. Probably using the vase. Afterall, the body doesn't bruise after death.

If Maxwell had been standing when he killed himself and fell and hit his head on the end table, he wouldn't have been found sitting with his back against the wall. He would have been found in a prone position on the floor.

Chapter 22

The Case of the Stinky Shoes

On the first day of vacation, which had fallen on a Saturday, Matt Perry awoke to the sunlight coming through his window.

All week had been warm as Spring turned into Summer. The weatherman stated today would be a real scorcher.

Matt got dressed and walked to the kitchen to eat breakfast. His wife, Muriel, sat at the table. She was drinking coffee and reading the morning paper.

"What's up, sleepyhead?" she asked, glancing up from the paper.

Matt wiped some sleep from his eyes. "Trying to make up for lost time." His stomach rumbled loudly.

"Someone's hungry," Muriel said. She set the paper down. "Would you like me to make you some eggs and toast?"

He pulled a chair out from the table and sat. "That would be lovely."

After making his breakfast, she brought him his plate and joined him back at the table.

She picked up the paper and flipped the page. "Hmm. This is interesting."

"What?" Matt asked, with his mouth full of eggs. He swallowed and chased it down with some orange juice.

Muriel glanced over the paper at him. He knew she didn't like it when he talked with his mouth full of food. He half expected her to say something. Instead, she said, "Someone left a pair of stinky shoes at the courthouse with a note that read, Justice Stinks."

"Did the police find out who did it?"

"Not yet. But the story goes on to say the note might have fingerprints, which could identify the criminal."

Matt wasn't sure a crime had actually taken place, except maybe littering because they left a pair of stinky shoes behind. But he wanted to know more.

"What else does the story say, Hon?"

"The police interviewed four people who were convicted of various crimes last week.

"The first was a businessman who trampled a newly fertilized flower garden. He was fined fifty dollars.

"A jogger was convicted of running across a busy intersection last week. Because he didn't use the crosswalk, two cars got into a fender bender. No one was injured in either vehicle. The jogger was sent to jail for ten days.

"A man in a wheelchair was found guilty of littering in the park. His lawyer pleaded for leniency. The judge took this under advisement and issued the man in the wheelchair a stern warning.

"The fourth was Baggy Britches the Clown who tripped a kid waiting in line to have a balloon made into an animal. The kid scraped his knee. The judge ordered the Baggy Britches to make the child a balloon giraffe."

Matt thought about each of the crimes and wondered which of them left the stinky shoes along with the note.

Matt smiled. "I know who did it."

Did you solve the case too? If not, turn to the next page to find out how Matt Perry solved the case.

Hint: That'll be a fifty-dollar fine.

The jogger was still in jail so he couldn't have left the shoes. The man in the wheelchair received a stern warning and the clown had to make a balloon animal.

This leaves the businessman, who was fined fifty dollars for trampling a newly fertilized flower garden. Fertilizer stinks which would have made the shoes smelly.

Acknowledgments

No writer can complete a book on their own without getting some help. I'm truly humbled by everyone who helped turn my idea Couch Detective into a reality.

The Panhandle Writers Group provides much needed feedback every Thursday. My editor, who wishes to remain anonymous continues to teach me. Also, my beta readers, Jane McFarland, and Helen Hall. You continue to keep me honest.

My wife is my biggest supporter and inspiration for all my projects. Without her, writing would be a dream, not a reality.

Finally, I'd like to thank you, the reader. I hope you enjoyed solving the cases and earning your title as Couch Detective. But if you didn't solve all of them before the end of each chapter, no worries. The next installment of Couch Detective is in the works.

About the Author

James Glass achieved the rank of Command Master Chief before retiring after 22 years in the United States Navy.

After retiring from the Navy, he exchanged his rifle for a pen. He and his family moved back to Florida.

James is also the President of the Panhandle Writers Group.

Checkout his website at www.jamescglass.com and discover his other books.

Made in the USA
Middletown, DE
26 March 2024

52112098R00089